DATE DUE		12/01
JAN 26		
OCT 28 '02		
MAR 30 05		

Rachel Captures the Moon

RICHARD UNGAR

Adapted from a story by Samuel Tenenbaum

Tundra Books

Published in Canada by Tundra Books,
481 University Avenue, Toronto, Ontario M5G 2E9

Published in the United States by Tundra Books of Northern New York,
P.O. Box 1030, Plattsburgh, New York 12901

Library of Congress Card Number: 2001086826

National Library of Canada Cataloguing in Publication Data

Ungar, Richard
    Rachel captures the moon

Adaptation of: Chelm captures the moon / Samuel Tenenbaum.

ISBN 0-88776-505-X

I. Tenenbaum, Samuel, 1902– . Chelm captures the moon. II. Title.

PS8591.N42R32 2001   jC813'.6   C2001-930076-X
PZ7.U53Ra 2001

We acknowledge the support of the Canada Council for the Arts and
the Ontario Arts Council for our publishing program.

We acknowledge the financial support of the Government of Canada through
the Book Publishing Industry Development Program for our publishing activities.

Design: Ingrid Paulson

Medium: watercolor and colored pencil on paper

Printed and bound in Hong Kong

1 2 3 4 5 6   06 05 04 03 02 01

For Rafi and Simon

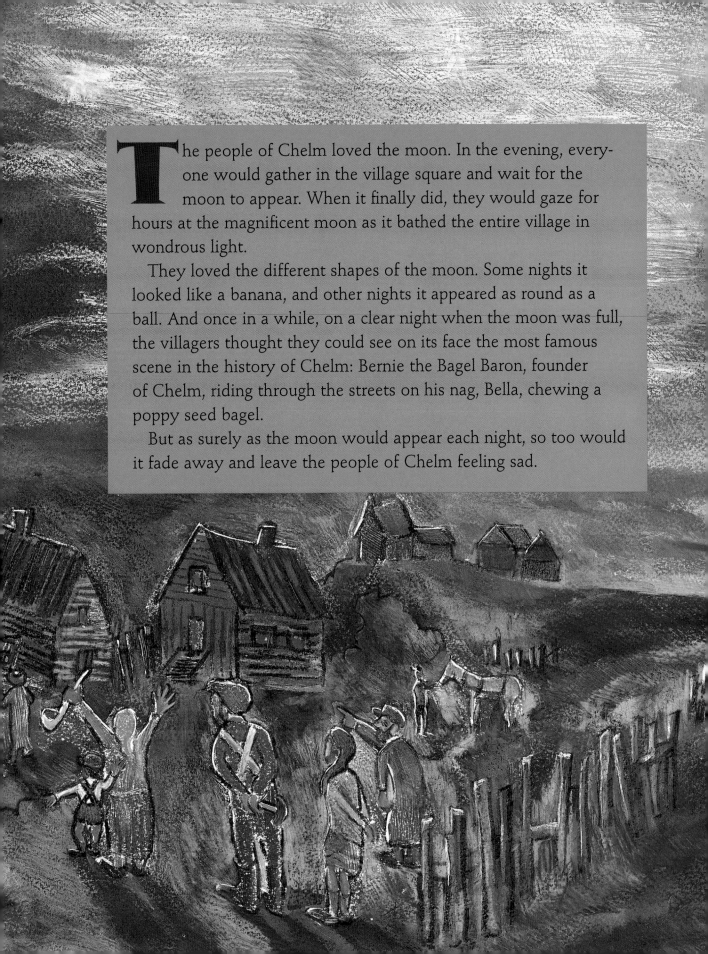

The people of Chelm loved the moon. In the evening, everyone would gather in the village square and wait for the moon to appear. When it finally did, they would gaze for hours at the magnificent moon as it bathed the entire village in wondrous light.

They loved the different shapes of the moon. Some nights it looked like a banana, and other nights it appeared as round as a ball. And once in a while, on a clear night when the moon was full, the villagers thought they could see on its face the most famous scene in the history of Chelm: Bernie the Bagel Baron, founder of Chelm, riding through the streets on his nag, Bella, chewing a poppy seed bagel.

But as surely as the moon would appear each night, so too would it fade away and leave the people of Chelm feeling sad.

One day, while working in his shop, Simon the Carpenter turned to his daughter and said: "Rachel, enough of this waiting for the moon to come out each night. I will capture it! That way we will all be able to gaze upon the moon at any time, day or night."

Simon had a plan. He built a ladder so high that he had to cut a hole in the roof of his shop to make room for it.

The following evening, Simon set his ladder against the side of one of the tallest houses in Chelm. At the first sight of the moon, Simon started climbing. He climbed higher and higher and higher. But try as he might, Simon could not reach the moon.

Next, it was Selma the Cook's turn. "The only way to capture the moon," announced Selma, busy at work in her kitchen, "is to tempt it with something that it cannot possibly resist. I have it! I will make a pot of my famous noodle soup. One whiff of my soup and surely the moon will dive down from its lofty perch to try some. When it does, I will quickly grab it!"

Everyone thought that Selma's plan was an excellent one.

That evening, Selma set a table in the middle of the village square. At the first sight of the moon, she lifted a bowl of steaming noodle soup high over her head. The delicious smell wafted up to the heavens. But try as she might, Selma could not entice the moon.

"I know of a sure way to capture the moon," proclaimed Rafael the Musician the next day, as he sat outside his small house, tuning his violin. "I will appeal to its love of music and play a beautiful melody. As soon as the moon comes near to hear my tune, I will snatch it from the sky!"

Everyone nodded approvingly. Rafael, they all knew, was the finest musician in all of Chelm. Surely Rafael would succeed and the moon would soon be theirs.

That evening, Rafael climbed to the top of the large hill just outside of Chelm. At the first glimpse of the moon, the sweet sounds of Rafael's violin filled the air. But try as he might, Rafael could not tempt the moon.

"I know!" said Sarah the Weaver, the next day. "What the moon really desires is to be warm. I will weave it a fine blanket. The moon will be so impressed that surely it will come down from the sky. When it does, I will wrap it so well in the blanket that it will not be able to escape!"

A perfect plan, everyone agreed.

That evening, in the village square, they all helped Sarah spread out the huge blanket swirling with many beautiful colors. They waited and waited, but still the moon didn't come down.

"All of you have it wrong!" shouted Aaron the Fisherman as he strode confidently through the streets of Chelm the following morning, his fishing net slung over his shoulder. "Catching the moon is like catching a big fish. It will battle until it is tired, and only when the fight has gone out of it can it be captured. Meet me on the pier this evening and you will see what I mean."

When the moon rose, everyone gathered on the pier and watched hopefully as Aaron walked past them to the very end. He stood there, motionless, for a very long time, watching the nearly full moon. Finally, at the precise moment that Aaron figured the moon must be very tired, he thrust his fishing net high into the sky. But try as he might, Aaron could not catch the moon.

The people of Chelm were beginning to lose hope. The next day, they gathered in the village square at sunset. Everyone was grumpy and no one spoke for a long time. Finally, a small voice called out: "Excuse me, everybody –"

"Rachel my child, this is not the time to bother us," Simon the Carpenter snapped impatiently. "We are conducting important business."

"But, Father," insisted Rachel, "I can capture the moon! Wait here."

Simon and the rest of the villagers groaned. "How can a child possibly succeed when everyone else has failed?" they wondered. But the people of Chelm desperately wanted to capture the moon. And so, they waited.

A few minutes later Rachel appeared, rolling a large rain barrel. With her every step, a little water escaped, sloshing onto the ground. When she finally arrived at the square, Rachel stopped and, with a grunt, lifted the rain barrel upright.

It was a clear night. At the first sight of the moon, Rachel motioned everyone to come closer so they could see into the rain barrel. "Behold, people of Chelm, the moon!" cried Rachel. And sure enough, there it was: their beloved moon, caught at last, inside Rachel's rain barrel! "Hooray for Rachel!" everyone cheered.

The villagers all agreed that capturing the moon was the greatest thing that had ever happened in Chelm. And, after considering the matter, they also agreed that the moon that Rachel had captured was even more magnificent than the one that filled the sky the following evening.